Kathryn Apel is a born-and-bred farm girl who's scared of cows. She lives among the gum trees, cattle and kangaroos on a Queensland grazing property, where she writes poetry, picture books and verse novels. Her previous books include *Bully on the Bus*, which won the Australian Family Therapists' Award for Children's Literature: Younger Readers, *Too Many Friends*, a CBCA Notable book, and most recently, *The Bird in the Herd*. Kat loves pumping poetry because she can flex her muscles across other genres, to bend (and break) writing rules. A trained teacher, Kathryn shares her passion for words at schools and festivals around the globe.

www.katswhiskers.wordpress.com

Also by Kathryn Apel

Bully on the Bus

On Track

Too Many Friends

The Bird in the Herd

what snail knows

Kathryn Apel

illustrations by
Mandy Foot

UQP

First published 2022 by University of Queensland Press
PO Box 6042, St Lucia, Queensland 4067 Australia

University of Queensland Press (UQP) acknowledges the Traditional Owners and their custodianship of the lands on which UQP operates. We pay our respects to their Ancestors and their descendants, who continue cultural and spiritual connections to Country. We recognise their valuable contributions to Australian and global society.

uqp.com.au
reception@uqp.com.au

Cover design by Jo Hunt
Cover and internal illustrations by Mandy Foot
Author photograph by F Apel
Typeset in 12.75/18 pt Adobe Garamond by Post Pre-press Group, Brisbane
Printed in Australia by McPherson's Printing Group

Queensland Government

University of Queensland Press is supported by the Queensland Government through Arts Queensland.

Australian Government | Australia Council for the Arts

University of Queensland Press is assisted by the Australian Government through the Australia Council, its arts funding and advisory body.

A catalogue record for this book is available from the National Library of Australia.

ISBN 978 0 7022 6546 4 (pbk)
ISBN 978 0 7022 6661 4 (epdf)

University of Queensland Press uses papers that are natural, renewable and recyclable products made from wood grown in well-managed forests and other controlled sources. The logging and manufacturing processes conform to the environmental regulations of the country of origin.

FSC www.fsc.org MIX Paper from responsible sources FSC® C001695

To Robyn S-B, who has quietly supported and set me on the right trail so many times in my (sometimes seemingly snail-slow) writing journey. I appreciate you.

Contents

our family

Just You and Me

'It's just you and me, Lucy,'
Dad said,
when all the other Prep kids
were making
Mother's Day cards,
and I asked,
'Where's my mummy?'

'It's just you and me, Lucy,'
Dad said,
when the Year One teacher
at a different school
wanted us to draw
our family tree,
and I asked,
'Why don't I have a
grandma and grandad?'

'It's just you and me, Lucy,'
Dad said,
when the Year Two teacher
at my last school
wanted Dad to update
my contact details.
'Because you were late,' I said,

'and we didn't know
who else to call.'

And when Dad and I
packed all our things
into our old brown car
(again),

Dad said
the same thing he'd
said every
time we'd
moved
before.
'It's just
you and me, Lucy. We
don't need nobody else.'

What If?

What if
it's just us
and I need
help?

What if
Dad gets sick
and I don't know
what to do?

What if
I can't help Dad
all by
myself?

What if
Dad isn't here?
Or Dad doesn't come?

If I'm alone …

What then?

And Snail

It isn't really
just
Dad and me.

Not anymore.

Now there's Snail, too.

That's his name.

Snail.

Hidden Treasure

I found Snail
not long after we moved in
to our other caravan –
before we moved to
this one.

I was walking around
the van park,
looking at my feet,
hoping to find
treasure.

And I did.

At first I thought it was
a shell.
I liked the brown and yellow
spiral stripes.

But when I picked it up
it was snail-heavy.

I perched on the step of our caravan,
with the shell sitting in
the palm of my hand.
Slowly, slowly, a sticky grey body
slid out …

Snail Trail

I made Snail a home
in a box –
from the recycling bin.
I put the box
under the caravan.

Snail escaped.

I was sad at first.

But Snail left
a message
in invisible ink.
A shiny trail.
For me to follow.
Across the concrete slab.

I was so glad when I found him.

I put Snail's box
beside my bed.
But when I wet the dirt a bit
(snails like that),
the cardboard went soft.
Made a puddle.
On the floor.

'You know Ol' Grumpy
in the office
won't like it
if we mess up
this dump,'
Dad grumbled.

Dad was gonna
toss the box …
(and Snail!)
But I said,

'That's Snail. My friend.'

And Dad huffed.
Rolled his eyes.

'Awww, Lu-cy …'

Us ... and Snail

Dad said we'd have to
find a box that didn't make
no mess.

We looked
at the op shop –
found a clear box
and matching green lid
with holes in it,
and a handle ...
and *$3* written
on the side
in pen.

But Dad said
he didn't have
that much money.

A shop lady said
it'd been sitting there
for months.

'You'll be doing us a favour
if you take it,' she said.

I carried Snail's new box
out of the shop
myself.

'We do all right, Lucy,' Dad said,
'just you and me.'

'And Snail,'
I said,

and smiled.

Moving House

I made
Snail's new box
into a home.

It's clear right through –
I can see Snail from
every side,
but not the bottom,
'cause I put dirt in it.
And leaf litter.
And even crushed eggshells –
to keep his shell strong.

Snail's new home
doesn't leak brown stains
onto the floor.

'It even *looks* like a snail home,'
Dad said, 'with those fancy holes up top
for breathing.'

So now Snail's got three homes:
his shell,
            his box,
                        our caravan.

And when we have to pack up
and move,

Snail is the first one ready

to go.

this place

Mei-hui

Mei-hui manages
the van park
where Dad and I
are staying.

She lives in a *real* house
behind the office.

Mei-hui sorts the mail,
collects the rent,
cleans the amenities block
(that's the showers and toilets),
and keeps the gardens
tidy
        and fresh.

She has heaps of gardens.

Mei-hui has the
best van park
we've stayed in.

She buzzes around
like a bee;
busy, busy, busy,
                    but nice.

'Take one.
Have a lolly, Lucy,'
she tells me,
when I go to
the office with Dad,
to pay our site fees.

One time she even gave me
an ice cream
from the little office shop.
And we didn't have
to pay for it.

Dad said it was okay …

'Just this once.'

Just Us

There's not much room
in a caravan,
so Dad and I go to
the parklands
a lot.

They're right beside
our van park.
There's a special gate
for residents to use,
that opens onto
the bamboo walk.

Mei-hui says
it's our gateway to
a secret garden.

On quiet afternoons,
I pretend the parklands
are our backyard.

Sometimes Dad pushes me
on the swings
and I sing like a bird.

Other times we look for treasure –
little flowers,
coins,
lost toys …
But on weekends,

there are people
everywhere.

'Watch this, Uncle Ben!'

'Jack! Put the lizard down!'

'Come push me, Grandad.'

They kick soccer balls,
play cricket,
throw frisbees
(and rubbish),
ride bikes,
scooters,
and rollerblades …

Laughing, arguing, eating …
spreading across the parklands
like a great big
shady
tree.

Sometimes I wonder why
our family
is just a seed,
when everyone else
has branches all over
their tree.

'What happened to
your mum and dad?'
I ask Dad.

'Are they still …
                    somewhere …?
Or are they with
                    my mum?

Do you miss them?'

Dad's hand brushes
across my head,
snagging
in my tangled hair.

'Ah, Lucy …
Where do these questions
come from?

I thought you were
happy
with your old dad?'

'You're not old,'
I tell him,
looking at the grandad
pushing the little kid
on the swing.

'That grandad is old.'

He Just Is

My dad is like a shadow.
        A whisper.
A hug.

His hair is
            a bit long,
            a bit brown,
            a bit curly,
            and a bit soft.

(It's a bit like mine –
except mine is lighter
and longer,
and because it hurts
when Dad tries to brush it,
my hair's always
            a bit knotty.)

People probably don't even
notice Dad's there.

                                    But I know.

Mum's the Word

Sometimes I think about
my mum.

Did she laugh a lot?
And sing songs?
And snuggle me
with kisses?

Did she know how
to brush knots out of hair,
then twist it into braids
and buns
with ribbons in them?

'Was my mum happy?'
I ask Dad.

'Your mum
could see the good
in everyone,
and make a rainy day
shine,'
Dad says,
looking into the distance.

He sighs.

'And then she was sick
and gone.

Too soon.'

Say What You Like

At school,
I usually try to find a place
away from other
kids.

It's better by
                myself.

Quieter.

I don't have to answer
other kids' questions.

But that doesn't stop them
talking about me.

  'She stinks.'

    'I don't think she
    brushes her hair.'

      'I saw her scavenging
      in the eating area.'

        They think I'm dumb.
          Can't hear them.
            Don't care.

But I'm not.
And I can.
And I do.

Secret Snail

Snail knows
that I don't like
always being
a new kid.

That I pretend
I don't notice
the whispers,
sniffs,
and laughs
when kids
turn their backs
on me.

That wearing
someone else's
faded old uniform
and shoes
with their stains
and smells
makes me
want to crawl inside
a shell …

and hide.

I Smell Trouble

Those kids probably don't know that:

1) Hand-me-down clothes
   have hand-me-down smells.
   So do old caravans.
   And old beds, too.
   So that smell?
   It isn't always me.

2) Clean clothes
   and dirty clothes
   start to smell the same
   if they're all in a muddle
   'cause there isn't much space.

3) It's easy to skip a shower
   when your dad's tired,
      or it's raining and cold,
         or you don't feel well …
   and the shower is a walk away.

4) Sometimes you forget
   to take
            the soap.

A Roof Over Our Beds

At least we
have a caravan
this time. Sometimes we sleep in
the car.

Snail Knows

That this new school
started
the same way –

until a kid called
Tahnee
squeezed
inside my shell.

Tahnee has
lots of friends.

I've never had
a friend before.

Except Snail.

I think Tahnee
might be
a friend.

I even went
to her birthday.
The whole class did.
Even the teacher.

I won a yo-yo.
A yellow one.
Snail knows I don't want
to break it.

School Rule

Even Tahnee
wants to know
stuff.

'Do you have any pets?'
'A snail.'
'What's its name?'
'Snail.'
'What does it look like?'
'A snail.'

But I don't always know
if I'm allowed
to tell.

'Did you like your old school?'
'Which one?'
'How many have you been to?'
'I can't remember.'
'Why did you move?'
I look away ...

Dad doesn't like it
when people get
too close.

‘We don’t need to know
their business.
They don’t need to know
ours,’ Dad says.

‘It’s just you and me, Lucy.
We don’t need nobody else.’

That’s why I sit
and watch

alone.

just one question

Nice One

The teacher at this school always
looks nice,
smells nice,
acts nice.

I think Snail would think
this teacher's nice,
too.

She wears nice clothes
that look like a garden.

How Can I Help?

On Monday morning,
the teacher has made a
new sign out of bright letters
that fill the classroom corkboard.

Who's that message for?
I wonder.

'How Can I Help?'
Roxie says,
reading the sign
aloud.
But it sounds like
she's trying to solve
a puzzle –
            not ask
            a question.

Oh, Help!

We're starting a new unit
of work.
That's what the teacher says.

She wants *us* to ask,
'How can I help?'
and she wants *us* to find ways
to help others.

I hope she doesn't
really want *me*
to *ask* people.

Maybe I can find ways
that people don't
notice,
and that don't cost
anything.

Who Needs Help?

'Who are we going to help, Miss?'
Jack asks.

'Let's start by helping at school,'
the teacher says.
'Any ideas?'

Roxie: We could pick up papers.
Jack: No way. I do litter duty all the time!
Heidi: You shouldn't break school rules, then.
Kody: My dad says there are too many rules.
Michael: Rules help keep us safe, Kody.
Sara: We could remind kids to wash hands.
Tahnee: I know … Let's make school rules cool!
Ashton: Yeah! Like: *Share and play fair.*
(Or beware!)
Pia: We could make cool school rule *posters!*

When we've finished,
the whiteboard looks like
crisscrossing snail trails
on a concrete path.
So many ideas
linked by lines;
but we all agree on
posters.

Oh, No – Group Work

The teacher pairs us all up –
even though
some kids want to choose
their own partners,
and everyone wants to choose
Tahnee.

'Work together
to brainstorm a
catchy phrase –
like Ashton's
Share and play fair.

Play with your words.

Your first attempt
might not be your
best effort.'

Silent Partner

I don't like group work.

But if I had to choose
a partner
I'd choose
Tahnee,
too.

Tahnee asks me
what I think.

Listens
when I talk …

Even if I don't
say much.

I'm glad
she's my partner.

Not Kody,
who'd complain.
Or Roxie.
Too bossy.
Or Jack.
Too jumpy!

I'm surprised
Tahnee's happy
with *her* partner.

Snails Know

'Let's do
walking on concrete,'
Tahnee says.

'Everyone forgets –
and then kids get hurt.'

I nod.
            It's true.

I've seen it
as I sit
and watch.

'We need to make the poster
fun … and catchy,'
Tahnee says,
'so kids remember.'

She starts scribbling down ideas.

> It's not fun to run.
>   Go slow.
> Walk and talk.
>   Feet _____ concrete
> Don't dent cement …

‘Snails know,’
I say.

‘Hmmmm?’

Tahnee waits.

‘Snails know to go slow,’
I say.

Tahnee grins
as her pencil slides
across the page.

More Snail Facts for Tahnee

gaStropod
omNivore
nocturnAl
invertIbrate
moLlusc

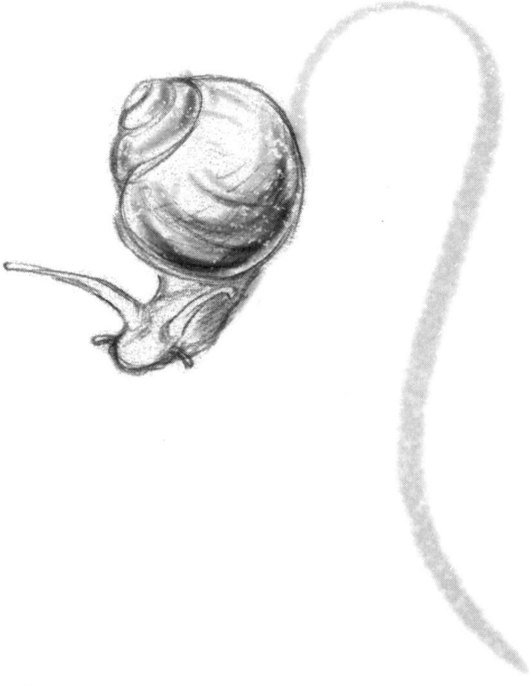

No Help Needed

I meet Dad
at the pick-up gate.

'What'd you do today?'
Dad asks, as we walk
to the van park.

(Sometimes we stop at
the parklands first.
But not this time.)

I tell him about
the teacher's big question.
How we're
helping others.

'Teacher says it's good
to help others.'

Dad grunts.

'Yeah.
That's all right.
But we don't need
no help, Lucy.'

I nod.
Because I know that.

Dad tells me.

All the time.

Working Things Out

I get my homework folder
and sit at the tiny table
in the part of the caravan
that is our kitchen.

I start to write out
my spelling words.

helping
washing
weeding
.
.
.

Dad is scrolling through his phone –
sometimes ringing people.

He's always looking
for work.

If he finds something
we might be able to stay
longer.

Shell-ter

Snail is sleeping.

I wipe inside his box
and put in fresh food
from school:

some apple
(from a *whole apple*
left in the garden),

banana peel
(I told Tahnee
Snail likes banana),

and a knob of cucumber
(Heidi didn't want it).

Then I spray water like dew
around his home.

Snail will be happy
when he wakes up.

Plan for Success

'Miss Darling,
we know what we want
to do for our poster,'
Tahnee says the next day.

She shows Teacher
our plan.

'Clever work, girls.
And I love that catchy phrase.'

'We worked together.'
Tahnee grins at me.

'Lucy knows a lot
about snails!'

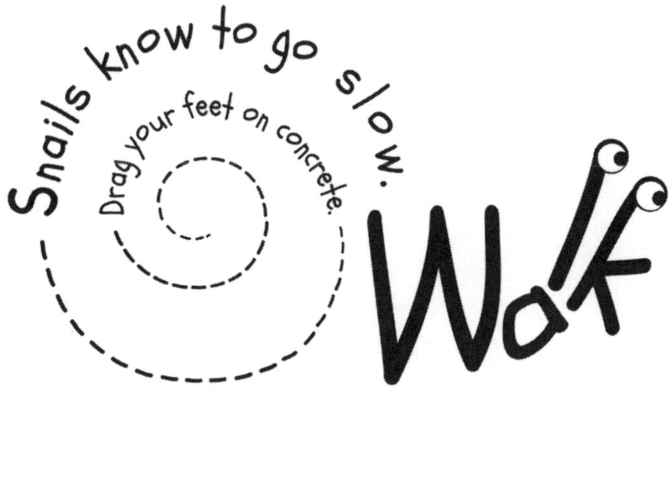
Snails know to go slow.
Drag your feet on concrete.
Walk

Roxie:	I wish Tahnee was my partner.
Jack:	That snail looks cool.
Heidi:	You're so clever, Tahnee!
Kody:	My dad says snails are pests.
Michael:	It looks good … but it's hard to read.
Sara:	The Preps will love that one.
Tahnee:	Lucy knows so many snail snippets.
Ashton:	That poster is slick – like a snail!
Pia:	Which part did you do, Lucy?

home helper

Wishy-washy

On Saturday,
Dad and I go to the
van park laundry
to do our washing.

Some of the resident kids
are playing cricket
with a tennis ball
in the middle of the road.

'Want to play, too?'
they ask.

But I shake my head
and keep walking.

If I play games
they'll ask questions,
and Dad doesn't like
people knowing
our business.

'Are you going to the pool later?'

'Maybe,' I say.
If Dad comes.

We fill the machine with
dirty clothes,
add the powder,
then feed coins through the slot.

Our washing sloshes and
swirls like a snail shell
as I ride my scooter
up and down the path,
and Dad tinkers under the
bonnet of our car.

It's not a very good car.
Sometimes it won't even start!
That's why we walk
everywhere.

'Can we get a new one, Dad?'

'Can't afford a new one, Lucy,'
Dad grunts,
reaching to wriggle a hose fitting.

'Can't afford the one we've got.'

Ashton Makes … Kids Laugh!

'How many of you
do jobs at home –
to help your family?'
the teacher asks on Monday morning.

'I make my bed,'
Ashton says.
'Every morning.
Without being reminded.'

'Well, that's good,'
the teacher says.
'But who is that helping?'

'My mum.'

'Oh?
Does she sleep in
your bed?'

Kids laugh.
Teacher's eyes sparkle.

'Miss Darling!
Of course she doesn't.
But if *I* make my bed
Mum doesn't have to.'

How Can I Help at Home?

'This week
we're going to be asking,
"How can I help?"
at home.

Not just helping
yourself,
          Ashton,

but helping others
in your family.'

                    'Making my bed
                    doesn't count?'

'No, Ashton.
Though you still
need to do that!

We're looking at ways
to help the family –
not just ourselves.

Thinking caps on …'

Things I Can Do to Help at Home

After we've brainstormed,
the teacher types
all our ideas
into a table.

	Mon	Tues	Wed	Thurs	Fri	Sat	Sun
set table							
hang up washing							
garden							
make another's bed							
make lunch							
wash car							
sweep floor							
feed pet							
read to sibling							
cook dinner							
walk dog							
wash up							
fold washing							
un/pack dishwasher							
clean toilet							
other							

'Your homework this week
is to do something
from the list
every day
to help at home.
Put a tick beside it
each time you do it.'

'I didn't think we had to do
homework on the weekend,'
Jack says.

Teacher rolls her eyes
and laughs.

'I don't think your parents
will mind, Jack,'
she says.

Home Work

Roxie: This week, it really is home *work!*
Jack: Can we cook toast? Does that count?
Heidi: What if we don't have a dog?
Kody: I hope Dad doubles my pocket money.
Michael: What if we don't know how to cook?
Sara: I have a purple folder full of recipes.
Tahnee: This homework will be fun!
Ashton: Yes, Miss … I'll still make my bed.
Pia: Whose idea was it to clean the toilet?

Easy as … Pie?

'Now we're going to look at
a recipe you could use
to cook dinner for your
family.'

Teacher hands out
a copy to everyone.

'This doesn't make any sense!' Jack says.

'Is this another joke, Miss?' Ashton asks.

Teacher hands me a sheet.

Sausage Pie.
Dad loves sausages
and eggs.
He'll like this.

But Jack's right –
it doesn't make sense!

'Are you sure this is
the right recipe, Miss Darling?'
Tahnee asks.
'It looks all muddled up.'

Teacher smiles.

'Good spotting!
You're *all* right –
the method is muddled.
Before we can make the pie,
you'll have to use the words
and picture clues
to order the recipe
correctly.'

'Miss Darling!'
Ashton groans.
'It really IS a joke!'

'A bad joke,' Michael grumbles.

The teacher reads through
the muddled recipe.

Then we each cut it up –
and try to put it
together …
          properly.

It's tricky.

Roxie finishes first.

'Try again, Roxie,'
the teacher says,

giving her a clue.

Every time someone
thinks
they've got it right,
Teacher finds something
wrong.

I watch …
and listen …
If I've made the same
mistake, I rearrange
my recipe …

Eventually,
Miss Darling reveals
the real recipe
on the big screen
so we can check
(and fix)
our work.

'Quick! Glue them down
before they blow away
and we have to start
again!' Roxie says.

I've read the instructions
so many times,
I think I know
what to do –

and what not to do!

Pie High

'Now, the fun bit,'
the teacher says.
We line up at the classroom door.
Follow Teacher
                    to the staffroom.
                    (What will the principal say?)

'I'm going to show you
how to make Sausage Pie,'
Teacher says,
'so you all know how to
do it yourself,
at home.'

        'What if we don't eat meat?'

'That's not a problem, Heidi.'
Teacher smiles.
'It works with
vegetarian sausages –
or you could chunky-chop
your favourite vegetables
instead.
It will still be yummy!'

Some kids have never used
a sharp knife,
or done any cooking.

I help Dad all the time.
If I don't,
who will?

Teacher shows us
how to be safe
with knives.

'There are no fingers
or thumbs
in this list of ingredients!'
she says.

'*Ewwwww. Gross.*'

Shop-Shape

'Can we go to the shops?'
I ask Dad
when he meets me at
the pick-up gate.

'I've already been,
Lucy-Lou,' Dad says.

He calls me that
when he's happy.

I smile.

I'm happy, too.
I like this school.
And teacher.

'I need to get these things,'
I say, showing Dad the recipe
that I chopped up,
rearranged
and glued together
the right way.

'Where'd you get this?'
Dad asks.

I tell Dad about
our homework.

'Your teacher's got
some funny ideas,'
he says,
shaking his head.

I hold my breath
as Dad frowns.
Starts to read.

I hope the things
on the list don't cost
much.

'Only thing we need to buy
is that puff pastry,'
Dad says.
'I got sausages
and eggs
and vegetables.

This week they'll be
pied
          not fried.'

I giggle.
Swing Dad's hand
as we turn towards
the shops.

'Looks like it's
your turn to cook,'
he says.

Pied Not Fried

After I've fed Snail, (✓)
I get everything I need
to make tea.

Dad sits at the table,
scrolling through his phone.

He's still looking
for work.

'Let me know
if you need any help,
Lucy-Lou,'
Dad says.

But I know exactly
what I have to do.

Ticking Boxes

Sausage pie (✓)
was easy to make and
yummy in my tummy.

'That's the best homework
you've ever had,' Dad says,
as we clean up. (✓)

I cut a chunk
for my lunch box,
wrap it in plastic,
put it in the fridge. (✓)

'I can cook it again
next week,' I tell Dad.

'You've got the job!' he says.

just like dad

Teacher … Miss Darling

On Tuesday
when I get to school,
the teacher
is inside the classroom.

'Teacher,' I say.

'Miss Darling,' she prompts,
with a smile.
'How can I help you, Lucy?'

'I made pie last night … Teach … Miss Darling.'

Miss Darling's eyes sparkle.

'That's wonderful, Lucy.
And was it
as tasty as mine?'

I lick my lips
and rub my tummy,
and Teacher …
Miss Darling …
laughs.

‘I even have some
for lunch
today,’
I tell her.

‘Snap!’
she says.
‘Me too!’

Checkmark Chores

During morning session,
Teach … *Miss Darling* … records
how kids have helped
at home.

The list of jobs is written
on the side of the whiteboard.
She puts a tally mark
for each time someone has done
a job.

'Next week,
we'll use all our data
to make a graph,'
Miss Darling says.

I wonder if there will be
any tallies beside
Clean the toilet.

'I'm making my sausage pie
on the weekend,' Roxie says,
'because Grandma and Grandad
are coming for lunch.'

'I'm sure they'll love that,'
Miss Darling says.

'And we will, too!'
says Roxie.

Pieces of Pie

Lots of kids have brought
cold sausage pie for
lunch – even
Heidi
.

Today, when all the kids
compare lunches,
I fit right
in
.

Jibber Jobber

All week Miss Darling
has been keeping a tally of jobs
we do.
And I keep doing the same ones
over and over
that I do all the time
anyway.

There's lots of jobs
I can't do
in a van park,
with no brother, sister,
dog, garden or dishwasher.

At least I can feed a pet (✓)

some carrot sticks
(left in the eating area),

a grape
(Jack threw at Tahnee),

and a nasturtium leaf
(Mei-hui says *we* can eat them, too).

Can I Help Mei-hui?

'Dad, if the van park
is our home …
        (for now),
can I help Mei-hui,
too?

Maybe I can
weed a garden …
or even
        clean the toilets?'

At first I think
Dad is going to say
                no,
but then he sees my
homework checklist,
hmphs
    and says,
'Okay.
But don't talk too much …'

I know what that means.

People don't need to know
our business.

Weekend Worker

On Saturday,
while our washing
snail-shell swirls,
I help Mei-hui
in the garden:
picking,
          planting,
potting and
          pruning.

Dad carts the clippings
to the compost bin.

When the machine
has finished swishing
and spinning,
Mei-hui sweeps the path
as I pass Dad pegs
and he clips our clothes
up to dry.

'Lucy, you are a good helper,'
Mei-hui says in her sing-song voice.
'Just like your dad.'

How We Roll

On Sunday afternoon,
Dad and I take the scooter
to the parklands
and I scoot along as Dad jogs.

Sometimes Dad scoots.

'I hope you don't
break it!'
I sputter
as I run along behind,
laughing.

'Did you have a scooter
when you were little?'
I ask Dad.

He grins.

'Nah – I had a skateboard.
Used to be like
those kids
hanging out there at
the skate park.

I knew some tricks
back in the day …'

‘We should see if
there’s a skateboard
at the op shop,’
I tell him.
‘Then we could both
have wheels!’

‘That’s how we roll,
Lucy-Lou,’
Dad says,

‘together.’

Lots of Gaps

On Monday,
my job tally looks like this:

	Mon	Tues	Wed	Thurs	Fri	Sat	Sun
set table	✓	✓	✓	✓	✓	✓	✓
hang up washing						✓	
garden						✓	
make another's bed	✓	✓	✓	✓	✓	✓	✓
make lunch	✓	✓	✓	✓	✓	✓	✓
wash car							✓
sweep floor		✓		✓			
feed pet	✓	✓	✓	✓	✓	✓	✓
read to sibling							
cook dinner	✓			✓		✓	
walk dog							
wash up	✓	✓	✓	✓	✓	✓	✓
fold washing						✓	
un/pack dishwasher							
clean toilet						✓✓ ✓✓ ✓	
other		✓	✓	✓			✓

'You can't clean the toilet
five times in one day,'
Roxie says.

'They're different toilets.'

'*We* don't even have
five toilets,'
Kody says,
'and Dad says ours is
the biggest house in town.'

'I helped Mei-hui
clean the ladies' toilet block,'
I mutter,
hunching down in my seat,
'at the van park.'

'That's not *your* toilet,'
says Michael.
'It doesn't count.'

'Who said this was a
competition?'
Miss Darling asks.
'I'm sure Mei-hui
was glad you helped, Lucy.'

'I made Mum's bed
every day!'
Ashton says.
'And mine, too.'

Kody's Dad Says Stuff

'My dad says
it's not your job
to teach us how to
cook and clean.

But Mum says
everybody should
know some recipes,
so I made sausage pie
for Saturday brunch
and even Dad said
it was good.'

talking rubbish

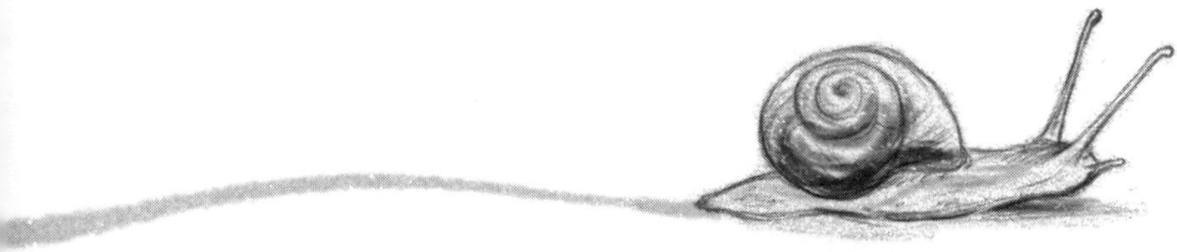

Local Tourist

Miss Darling shows us
a slideshow of photos
she took on the weekend.

'I know that place!' Jack says,
when the parklands
appear on the screen.
'There's a playground
near there
          and paths
                    and gardens.'

'What else do you notice?'
Miss Darling asks.

'Rubbish spilling out of the bins,'
Tahnee says. 'It looks awful!'

(It smells awful, too!
                              I know.
That's the bin where we found
                              my scooter.)

'That's the playground near
Dad's place,' Heidi cries,
when Miss Darling flicks
to a new photo.

Looking closely, I see
scrunched-up
fast-food packaging,
and empty drink bottles
lying in the sand.

'Is that the dump?'
Michael asks,
when Miss Darling switches
to another photo.

'Why were you taking
photos around town?'
Heidi asks.

'And so many photos
of rubbish?'
asks Roxie.

'This week we're looking
for ways to help
our community,'
Miss Darling says,
'and our community has
too much rubbish!'

PIEces of Rubbish

Michael says
we should do a survey
and see what rubbish
kids have in their lunch boxes.

We ask each class
to save their lunch litter
and we organise it into:

- plastic
- paper
- tin
- food.

(I take my food scraps
home for Snail.
That's not rubbish.)

We make a pie graph
on the concrete
using actual rubbish!

'I wouldn't want to eat
that pie!' Jack says.

I agree.
It looks disgusting!

Although,
Snail might like it …

If I Was a Worm

'Food isn't really rubbish,'
Pia says.
'We shouldn't be throwing it
in the bin.'

Pia is right.
Kids throw away
too much good food.

(And too much junk food!)

I often sneak snacks
for Snail
from food that kids
have wasted.

'If we had a worm farm
we could be making soil
for the garden,' says Michael.

'My mum says
composting is better
than worm farms,'
Heidi says.
    'Less mess.'

'They're both great options,'
Miss Darling says, writing them
on the board.

Not Wrapped in Plastic

On Tuesday,
we're still talking about
ways to reduce rubbish.

'My cousin's school had a
plastic-free day
where kids were encouraged
to NOT wrap their lunch
in plastic,' Sara says.

'But is one day enough?'
Miss Darling asks.

It's Rubbish to Litter

We research how much
waste is discarded each year.
Discover islands
made of floating plastic!
Learn how our plastic is harming
sea creatures.

Turtles think
plastic bags are jellyfish.
Food! But when swallowed,
the bags get stuck inside and the

t s s
u l t
r o a
t w r
l l v
e y e
s .

Dad and I saw
baby turtles when we were living
near the beach;
hatchlings erupted out of the sand

then flipper-flapped
like little wind-up toys
as they floundered down
to the foaming water …

My Turtle Trap

I had a lunch box once.

But it got left behind
one time we moved –
now I just
use plastic wrap
and carry my lunch
in a plastic bag.

My plastic
could be floating
out into the ocean
like jellyfish …

What am I going to use
if I don't use plastic?

We don't have money
for containers.

It's a Wrap!

'Maybe we could use paper bags
or sandwich paper
instead of plastic,'
Pia says.

I like that idea.
Maybe Dad can buy some.

'Miss Darling,
my mum makes us
beeswax wraps,'
Tahnee says.
'You use them
over and over again.
Do you want me to ask
if she can show us how to make our own?'

Roxie: Oh, I love Tahnee's lunch wraps!
Jack: They've got hearts all over them.
Heidi: That's because they're the Hart family.
Kody: My dad says I don't use much plastic.
Michael: What if we can't make one at home?
Sara: My gran has lots of material I could use.
Tahnee: Mum could help make them at school!
Ashton: Let's ask her, Miss. It's a wrap!
Pia: Ashton, you are un*bee*lievable!

I feel my lips tease into a smile …
that grows into a grin
when Miss Darling
says we can write to
Tahnee's mum
and ask.

This school is
the best school
I've ever been to.

A Gym for Him

In the afternoon,
I sit in the shade and
watch Snail slide slowly
through the jungle gym.
(That's what I call the garden
beside our caravan.)
Snail's eye-stalks
arc and sway
like they're dancing.
So much to see!

'You want to stay here, too,
don't you, Snail?' I murmur,
arranging fresh twigs and stones
into a sliming gym
inside Snail's home.

'Tahnee says
she wants to meet you.

I think
you'll like her.'

Dad
bangs and clangs under
the bonnet of the car. For ages!

'Do you think you can get it going?'
I ask, as he wipes his hands on a
greasy rag, then leans through
the driver's door.

Turns the key.
Car splutters.
Dad mutters.
No go.

'Maybe it won't
ever start
and we'll be
stuck
here,
Snail
.'

Yes!

Tahnee's mum said
yes,
she can come in and show us
how to make beeswax wraps,
    and *yes,*
she could certainly help us
make our own,
        and *yes,*
she has enough resources,
so would this Friday
suit Miss Darling …?

And Miss Darling says,
'Yes.'

'YES!'

Bee Mine

On Friday,
Mrs Hart brings a stack of fabric,
and we get to choose
which one we'll use
for our beeswax wraps.

'Look, Lucy!' Tahnee cries,
waving a brightly patterned piece.

'Snails!'

Get Rapt in Wraps

What You Need:

- 100 per cent cotton cloth
- grated beeswax
- coconut oil
- baking paper
- pinking shears
- iron.

What You Do:

1) Cut a 20 centimetre square of cotton cloth.
   Pinking shears look like crocodile teeth.
2) Lay the cloth on a large sheet of baking paper.
   Save the ironing board.
3) Smear coconut oil over the cloth.
   It makes your hands soft.
4) Sprinkle beeswax across the cloth.
   Now it looks like a cheese pizza.
5) Lay a large sheet of baking paper on top.
   Save the iron.
6) Heat iron on a low setting, then
   press gently onto the beeswax wrap stack.
   Mind your beeswax spreads to the edge.

7) Remove baking paper while wax is warm, then hold the wrap by the corners until …
Cool!

Snail will be rapt.

I Tell Dad

'Everyone got to choose
their material.
Look, mine has snails on it.

And it smells like honey!

We all got to take
our own home.

And I don't have to give it back.

It's mine.
Forever.
For my lunch.
Next week.
And every week.

It's not rubbish!

Don't throw it in the bin!'

Pick Me Up

Dad says
he has news, too;
he's got a job
picking fruit.

Not a forever job, but …

'It's good money, Lucy-Lou.
And the season is just
beginning.'

To celebrate,
we're having takeaway:

fish and chips!

My tummy's rumbling
and we haven't even
ordered yet.

Saturday Rocks

We bundle
up our dirty clothes
and head to the
van park laundry.

A group of the resident kids
are sitting at the barbecue area,
with rocks and paint and brushes
and newspaper covering
the picnic table.

'Want to join us?'

I slow down …

'What are you making?'

'Happy rocks,'
says the biggest girl.
'Mei-hui said we can put them
in the gardens.'

Dad and I always do
our weekly washing
together, but …

'Want to paint one?'
the girl asks.

I look at Dad.
He doesn't answer
straightaway.

'It's helping
to make the park
friendlier,' I say.

Dad raises his eyebrows.
A smile twitches his lips.
'I can probably handle
the washing today.'

I pile the pegs and powder
on top of his washing bundle,
and scoot onto the seat
beside the girl.

'Do you know what you'd
like to paint?' she asks.

I do!

Rock This Place

After lunch,
our happy rocks are dry.

'These are so, so good,'
Mei-hui says,
beaming at us
as she turns each one over
in her hands.

'A snail?'
Mei-hui frowns.
'I don't know …
A snail …
In the garden …
Eating all the plants?'

But then she laughs,
and a smile slides
across my face.

'This snail
will not each much,'
Mei-hui says.

My Treasure

I run to the caravan
to show Dad my rock …

He's working on
the car, again –
needs to get it going
so he can drive to work
on Monday.

'Does it start?'
I ask.

I hope it does.

If Dad has work
he might want to stay
longer.

I want to stay!

He turns the key
and the car shudders …
                                        to a start.

'High five, Lucy-Lou,' Dad says.

We slap hands,
then

I run off
to join the other kids
giggling and chattering
as they plant happy rocks
in little nooks
around Mei-hui's gardens.

It feels like
a treasure hunt …
but we're hiding
the treasure.

Snail Snack

On Sunday,
I make
sausage pie
again –
but this time I add
capsicum, parsley
and tomato that
Mei-hui grew
in her garden.

I want to take
sausage pie to school
in my new snail-print beeswax wrap!

I wrap Dad's pie in plastic
but remind him
to put his rubbish
in the bin.

'Next time we shop
we have to buy you
paper lunch wrap,'
I say.

getting the jump on toads

Pick-up Picker

On Monday,
Dad drives me to school
for early drop-off,
so he can get out and start
picking.

'See you this afternoon,'
he calls through the open window,
as I walk through the gate.

'You'll be the sweetest thing
I pick all day, Lucy-Lou.'

Frog and Toad

Over the weekend,
pictures of toads appeared
on the 'How Can I Help?' corkboard.

'Miss Darling, you do know
that if you want to find
a handsome prince,
you kiss a *frog* …
                    not a toad,'
Ashton says.

'Oh? Is that what happened
to you?' Miss Darling asks,
with a sparkle in her eyes.

'Miss Darling,
I am not a frog!'
Ashton splutters.

'No – I think your mum would say
you're a handsome prince,'
Miss Darling says.

'More like a toad,' Jack jokes.

Ashton groans –
but he's laughing, too.

Toadally Not Okay

Roxie:	Why do you have all the toad pictures?
Jack:	Toads aren't helping the environment.
Heidi:	Do you want us to help *toads?!?!*
Kody:	My dad says toads are *pests!* Not pets.
Michael:	I'll help get *rid* of toads!
Sara:	We have heaps of toads. *Urgh!*
Tahnee:	Toads have feelings. We can't *hurt* them.
Ashton:	My lips are sealed about frogs. And toads.
Pia:	Miss, do you know about toad busters?

'Toad busting,' Jack says.
'That sounds like fun!'

'Let's see what we can find out
about toads,' Miss Darling says.

'And toad busters,' Jack adds.

'We'll jump right in with these
fun facts,' Miss Darling says,
as she picks up a magazine
and starts to read.

Rhinella Marina: What Is It?

It starts as an egg
in a long sticky strand
but is born in water
and not on land.
It has no legs,
just a body and tail,
but it's not a fish
and it has no scale.

It feeds on algae
as it wriggles about
and before too long,
its back legs sprout!
Some waterweed
to nibble and eat …
And what do you know?
There's two front feet!

It looks like a frog,
but it paddles all day,
until the tail
has shrunk away.
Then one cool night
it clambers out

to join a group
and hop about.

It swam as a tadpole,
but now it jumps,
in a leathery skin
that's covered in bumps,
with a bony plate
inside its head
and poison glands
that leave things dead.

It isn't native –
it was introduced,
but now it's spread
and mass-produced.
It is a pest
that must be slowed.
Rhinella Marina …
It is a toad.

Toad Buster Muster

'That's what the toad buster group does,'
Pia says.
'They catch cane toads
to control the spread.'

Miss Darling nods.
'Toad busting is a way
we could help our community
and our environment.'

'I'm not touching toads!' Roxie says.

We have loads of toads
at the van park.
They hop into the amenities block
if someone leaves the
door   open.

One night
one jumped
into my shower!

I shudder.

I'm not touching toads, either!

The Kiss of Death

Miss Darling says
it isn't safe
to handle toads
because toxins ooze
from their poison glands
onto their skin.

'That's why
you shouldn't *kiss* a toad, Miss,'
Ashton says, grinning.
'Toads are toxic.'

Miss Darling rolls her eyes.

'It's also why native animals
          – and pets –
get sick … or die,
if they eat
          – or play with –
toads,' she says.

Miss Darling passes books
and brochures about
cane toads
around the class.

'Oh no,' Tahnee cries,
looking up from the book she is reading.
Looking at me.
'It says that *toads* eat *snails*.'

I gasp.

'What are you worried about?'
Kody says.
'Snails are pests.'

Kody thinks he knows
everything –
but he's wrong about snails.

'Snails are little vacuum cleaners.'
I blurt out.
'They help clean up
the environment –
and their poo is
plant food.'

Kody snorts.

'Well, they eat my dad's orchids –
so they're pests.'

'Snail shells are
an important source of calcium
for other animals,' Miss Darling says.

I shudder,
scrunch my eyes,
and try not to imagine
those poor snails.

'But, Miss Darling,' Heidi puzzles,
'how does the snail live,
without its shell?'

Kill Toads Kindly

Miss Darling shows us a website
where the RSPCA
says you can refrigerate toads
to put them to sleep,
                                        then freeze them …
                                                        to death.

And it doesn't hurt them.

'Eeeeeew!'

          'That's disgusting!'
'Toads in the freezer!'
          'Mum would crack!'
'My dad would never allow that.'
          'I don't think this is a good idea, Miss.'
'I think this is a bad idea, Miss.'
          'Oh, dear … Poor toads.'
'They're hopping mad!'
          'Ice cream would never be the same.'

(We all agree we will NOT be putting
toads in *our* fridges … or freezers!)

'I suggest we email Pia's toad buster group,'
Miss Darling says,
'since they're already set up to
kill toads kindly.'

Knots of Toads

'We were at the parklands
last night, and there were
lots of toads,' Roxie tells the class
during morning session
on Wednesday.

'Knots. Not lots,'
Michael says.
'A group of toads
is called a knot:
k-n-o-t.'

'Well, it was *not* a good idea
to bring *knots* of toads
to Australia!' Roxie declares.

'We won't make
that mistake again,'
Ashton says.

Miss Darling's eyes crinkle in concern.

'I wish that were true, Ashton,'
she says, 'but we already have.'

'What do you mean?'
Jack asks.

'I didn't make any mistakes,'
Michael mutters.

'Toads aren't
the only creature
introduced into Australia
to get out of control
and endanger native animals,'
Miss Darling says.

Place Invaders

Jack wants to
know more about
invader animals –
but Miss Darling says
that's a good topic
for him to research
later.

'For now,
we have an email
from the toad buster group.

'Yaaay!'
          'Hurray!'
                    'What did they say?'

Hop to It!

Dear Year Two,

We're pleased to hear you're
helping others … and our environment.

Toads are an introduced invasive species,
poisoning native wildlife and spreading
across Australia.

We must arrest the pest!

Toad Busters meet at 7pm
on the first Friday of the month
at the parklands.

You catch. We kill … kindly.

Everyone is welcome to jump on board.
But kids, bring an adult with you.

Let's hop to it!

Roger

Helping or Not

'The first Friday of the month?
That's next week,' Pia says.

'Can we do it?' Ashton asks.

I really don't want to touch a toad …

But they are doing so much damage.

This is a good way to help our
community –
and our environment.

And Snail.

When Miss Darling asks
who is keen to come,
I put up my hand …

Risk Assessment

'But, Miss,
if toads are toxic,
how are we going to
catch them?'

'Great question, Heidi.'

We identify risks
        and how to reduce them.

1) *Poison on our hands:*
   - *wear gloves*
   - *use grabbers*
   - *make a scoop.*

2) *Poison in our eyes:*
   - *wear goggles or glasses*
   - *keep hands (and gloves) away from eyes*
   - *don't look into their eyes* (Jack).

3) *Poison in our mouths:*
   - *don't kiss a toad* (Ashton)
   - *keep hands (and gloves) away from mouth*
   - *wash hands well after toad busting.*

We list the gear we'll need.

- *goggles*
- *gloves*
- *grabbers*
- *torch*
- *bucket*
- *scoop*

Inside Scoop

Miss Darling tells us,
'Your homework
is to design and create
a toad scoop
using at least one
plastic milk bottle.

You have until Friday next week
to make it.

Successful scoops will
pick up a toad
          without you touching –
                    or hurting –
                              it.'

Roxie: Tahnee, let's start at lunchtime!
Jack: I'll make a super-scoop and catch heaps!
Heidi: Can parents help?
Kody: If Dad helps, we'll make the best scoop.
Michael: You've got to draw a proper plan first!
Sara: I think we all know that, Michael.
Tahnee: Ella and I love making things at home.
Ashton: ♫ *Scoop-a-dee-doo-dah.*
Scoop-a-dee-ay. ♫
Pia: What if we don't drink milk, Miss?

‘I can bring in
extra milk bottles, Pia.
Yes, a plan is important,
Michael.
Adult (and big sister) helpers
are a great idea,
especially when cutting containers.
Just remember –
it’s *your* project!’

falling down

It's Just ... **Me**

In the afternoon,
I wait
at the gate
but Dad's late.

The pick-up area
is empty,
the school is quiet,
even some of the teachers
have left
and

it's just … me …

Dad doesn't come.

'Lucy! You're still here,'
Tahnee cries,
running up from the playground.

'I didn't know you were here.

Is your dad at the P & C meeting?'

I don't know anything about
a meeting –
and Dad would never leave me
waiting this long …

I shake my head,
stare down the street
as far as my eyes
can see.

Is that Dad?
Is he coming?

Or

is

it

just

a

wheelie bin?

Waiting …

Tahnee is back
and I didn't even know
she was gone.

'Is Dad running late?'
Miss Darling asks.

I shrug. But I don't
look away.
Don't want to miss
seeing Dad.
Don't want worry
to squeeze out my eyes
and slide down my cheeks.

'Maybe Dad got caught up
at work. Come back
to the classroom
and you can wait there,'
Miss Darling says.
'You and Tahnee
can help me tidy the room
until Dad gets here.'

'But Dad is never late like this!'
I tell Miss Darling.

Maybe the car stopped.
And his phone won't work.

'Don't fret, pet,' she says,
smoothing her hand over my hair.
It doesn't tangle
in the knots
like Dad's hand does.

Why won't Dad come?

Miss Darling's hand
slides down to my shoulder
as she
guides me
up the path
towards the classroom …

'We'll try and call Dad,'
she says.
'Or maybe a friend?
I won't leave until someone comes.'

'It's just Dad and me …'
I whisper.

So why won't he come?

Time Ticks By

Tahnee's mum
has finished her meeting
and my dad
still
isn't
here.

Miss Darling
and Mrs Hart talk quietly
as Tahnee buzzes around
tidying the classroom
and I …
                    wait.

I try to help.
But I can't help *worrying*
about Dad.

Worried Sick

Miss Darling and Mrs Hart
ask me
lots of questions
about Dad's new job:

'Where does he work?'
'An orchard.'
'What's its name?'
'I don't know.'
'What's he picking?'
'Oranges.'
'Who does he work with?'
'I don't know.'
'When did he start?'
'Yesterday.'
'Which way is the orchard?'
'I don't know.'
'What type of car does Dad drive?'
'A brown one.'

I'm worried
that Dad will think they know
too much about
our business.

But I'm more worried
about my
dad.

Comfort Snail

Miss Darling
            and Mrs Hart
have stepped outside –
are on their mobiles,
calling orchards around town,
asking if anyone knows
my dad.

Tahnee has found a book
about snails.

She sits close,
our shoulders
touching.

Reads it to me.

Because I can't concentrate
on words
today.

I'm not really listening
or looking –
until I see a photo
of …

'Snail,' I say,
pointing at the photo.

'That one
looks just like
Snail.'

Tahnee leans closer.
Looks carefully.
Traces her finger
around the spiral stripes
on the shell.

'He's beautiful, Lucy,'
she says.

Finders Keepers

Miss Darling crouches
close beside me –
I peer at her face,
          looking
for Dad.

'Did you … find him?'

Miss Darling's eyes
shimmer as she nods.

'Dad fell off a ladder today,'
she says.
'He banged his head
and was a bit confused –
didn't even realise
school had finished.'

'But he knows now?'
I ask Miss Darling.
'He's coming to get me?'

'They want him to stay in hospital
tonight – to make sure
everything is okay,' Miss Darling says.

'Is there a bed there,
for me?' I ask.

'Dad won't want me
at the caravan
by myself.'

Miss Darling reaches out.
Holds my hand.

'Of course he wouldn't, honey.
Mrs Hart says you can have
a sleepover
          with Tahnee …'

I jump up.
Shake my head.
Grab my bag.
Try to run …

But Miss Darling is holding tight
to my hand
and won't let go.

'It's all right, Lucy,'
she says.
'You've been
to Tahnee's house before …
For Tahnee's party, remember?

And Tahnee is a good friend to you
at school …'

'I know. But …

It's just Dad and me,' I say,
jiggling on the spot
with the worry
in my feet.

'We don't need nobody else.

Dad says so!'

Shhhleep Talking

Miss Darling
calls the hospital,
and I talk to Dad.

He's hard to understand –
his words smoosh together
and tangle on his tongue,
a bit like when I wake him
in the night to take me
to the toilets.
                    But worse.

'If Mrshrsh Har … t
takesh care of … you,
I'll conshentrate … on getting
better,' Dad slurs.
'We'll be together … shooon,
Lushy …'

He's already snoring
when Miss Darling
presses *End*.

A Coil of Concern

My worries
are still swirling
around and around
inside my tummy
like …

'Snail!' I cry.
'Who will look after Snail?'

Tahnee's mum
looks from me to Tahnee
to Miss Darling.

'Snail is Lucy's pet snail,'
Tahnee explains.

'I feed him every night.

Who will look after Snail
if Dad and I aren't there?'

Mei-hui Helps

Mei-hui is in the rose garden
near the park office
when we arrive.

'Oh, my sweet Lucy,'
Mei-hui says,
when Mrs Hart tells her
about Dad.

Her eyes are
as soft
as the touch of
her hands.

'He is a good father.
Always taking
care of Lucy.'

Mei-hui smiles
at Tahnee and her
big sister, Ella.
'Tonight you will take
care of our Lucy … yes?'

Made for Me

'I'll help you pack a bag,'
Mrs Hart says,
unlocking the caravan
with Mei-hui's spare key.

We sort through a
pile of clothes
until we find
a clean uniform
and pyjamas.

I get my toothbrush, too.

'I don't have another bag …'
I say.

Mrs Hart sends Tahnee out to get
a cloth shopping bag
from the basket in the boot.

'Look! It's the same material
as your beeswax wrap,'
Tahnee says.
'That's why I chose it.'

‘It must be made for you, Lucy,’
Mrs Hart says, as she helps me
fold my things
and fit them into the bag.

Snail is already packed.

I carry his box
to the car,
as Mrs Hart
locks our caravan,
then Ella runs the key
back to the office.

‘Bye, Mei-hui!’
Tahnee calls,
as we drive

away.

Holiday House?

Tahnee shares a bedroom
with Ella.

It's bigger
than our whole caravan.

There's a bed
under Tahnee's
that they pull out
for me to sleep on.

'Where do you live
when you're not at
the van park?'
Ella asks.

'I don't know where
we'll live, next time,'
I say.

'Is it like your holiday house?'
Ella asks.

'No, silly,'
Tahnee says.
'That's where she *lives!*'

So Many Choices

'Let's work on our toad scoops,'
Tahnee says, getting notepads –

'Do you want one with
balloons …
or puppies …
or maybe you'd like this
flower one …?'

– and a rainbow of
colourful pencils and pens,
erasers (that look like toys),
rulers,
a sharpener,
scissors …

More stuff than we need!

At the caravan,
I'd use the pencil from my
homework folder
and write on the back of a
scrap of paper –
maybe a docket or flyer –
or a page that Dad would carefully
pull out of my homework book.

'I hope we can make
our scoops
before your dad
gets out of hospital,'
Tahnee says.

I like drawing with Tahnee.
But I hope my dad
comes home
soon.

Steak – No Mistake

For dinner, Tahnee's mum
          makes a salad
and her dad
          cooks the meat.
Steak.
          Real steak.

I hope Dad
has steak
in the hospital.

He likes steak –
but we don't get it
much.

Dad says it costs
an arm and a leg.
Sausages just cost
a finger
          and a toe.

Appealing Pets

After dinner,
Tahnee's mum gives me
some salad scraps
for Snail.

Snail is still
tucked inside his shell.
I think he's shy.
Tahnee's house is a lot
noisier than our caravan.

'So, ummmm …
What do you do
with a pet snail?'
Ella asks,
as she scoops a
sleepy orange cat
off her bed
and into her lap.

'Feed it,' I say.

'And talk to it.

Watch it.

Snail sleeps a lot.'

‘Sounds a bit like a cat,’
Ella says.

‘I don’t think Snail is as
fussy as Banjo,’
says Tahnee.

‘Or bossy.’ Ella grins.

Sleep Thinking

At bedtime,
Tahnee and Ella
whisper
          and giggle
in the dark.
But I lie there thinking
of
Dad
by himself
in the hospital.

Is he missing me?
                    Does he hurt?
Is he worried?
          Will he be better soon?

'Girls,
no more chatter,'
Mr Hart says,
pausing at the doorway.
'Let Lucy get some sleep.'

'She's already asleep,'
Ella whispers.

Soon, Tahnee and Ella
are breathing slow
and steady.

But I'm still thinking.

Does this mean
the Hart family
know too much?
That Dad and I
(and Snail)
will have to move

again?

Catnapping

When I wake up,
Banjo is curled at the
bottom of my bed.

'He likes you, Lucy,'
Tahnee says.

It's later than Dad and I
would wake up
at the caravan.
I wonder how we'll
get our lunches made
in time for school.

But when we go to the kitchen
for breakfast,
there are three fancy lunch boxes
sitting packed and ready
on the bench.

'There's homemade
sausage roll,
berry muffin,
carrot sticks and dip,
popcorn,
kiwifruit

and an apple,'
Mr Hart says.

I don't know which
to choose.

'Ummmm …
Sausage roll
            and apple?'
                        I say.
(I'll save the apple core
for Snail.)

'Oh, you don't have to choose,'
Mrs Hart says,
handing me a very heavy lunch box.
'It's all packed,
so there should be
something there you'll like.'

'Ummm …
I won't waste it,'
I tell her,
sliding it into my backpack.

It feels like there's enough
for Dad *and* me!

On Call

While we're eating breakfast,
Tahnee's mum calls
the hospital
to see how Dad is
today.

'Lucy,
someone wants to talk
to you,' she says,
handing me
her phone …

'Hello? Lucy?'

'Dad!' I cry,
hugging the phone
close to my ear.
'You sound heaps better!'

'I'll be coming home today,' he says.

Sharing Care

'I'm sure you'll take
good care of your dad,'
Miss Darling says,
when I tell her
he's coming home.

'We always look after
each other,' I say.

'And Snail, too.'
(I hope he'll be all right today
at the Harts' house.)

Tahnee grabs my hand.

'Come on, Lucy,'
she says.
'Mei-hui asked me
to look after you,
remember?'

Class Can't Contain Themselves

Mrs Hart is waiting outside
the classroom door
when the home bell rings.
She's holding the snail-print bag
that matches my
snail-print beeswax wrap.

In the other hand, she's holding …

Roxie:	What's in the container, Mrs Hart?
Jack:	Is that for our classroom?
Heidi:	I hope it's not a tarantula!
Kody:	My dad says a tarantula would be cool.
Michael:	Do you want me to carry something?
Sara:	Michael. Stop pushing!
Tahnee:	I told you Mum wouldn't forget, Lucy.
Ashton:	I think she forgot the fish though.
Pia:	A fish doesn't live in dirt, Ashton.

'Snail!'

I smile at Mrs Hart.
'You remembered.'

Another Adult

Mrs Hart
helps me fit the
snail-print bag
into my backpack.
'If we've missed anything,'
she says,
'Tahnee can bring it to school.'

'I'll look after your bag,'
I tell her,
'and give it back tomorr—'

I forget what I am saying
and doing …

I forget that
Snails know to go
                                        s l o w.

I forget everything
          and run
down the path,
straight to
my dad.

no more

As Tight as a Squeeze

Dad hugs me tight.
I squeeze him tighter.

So tight, tears swim
around our eyes,
and I forget
we're still at school.

Food for Thought

'I missed you!
  Are you really better?
    Where did you get hurt?

      Can we go home now?'

'We'd better get your things first,'
Dad croaks,
then clears his throat
and wipes his knuckles
across his eyes.

I look back to where
Tahnee and Mrs Hart
are waiting
by the port racks,
holding my backpack –
and …
      'Oops.
      I forgot Snail.'

Tahnee giggles.

'Hey. Thanks for
looking after Lucy,'
Dad says,
as Miss Darling joins us.

'I guess my head
isn't as hard as I
thought …

But I'm good now.'

Mrs Hart tells Dad that
I was
no trouble –
and welcome over any time.

'And Snail, too,'
says Tahnee.

Dad shoves his hand
through his hair
and looks at me.

'She's a good kid.
But we're pretty right,
just the two of us.'

Mrs Hart hands Dad
a soft esky
full of yummy smells.

'I'm sure you want to get
home
and rest up.

We cooked you some
soup and snacks.
Enough for tea tonight
and lunches tomorrow.'

Dad starts to shake his head.

'Oh. You shouldn't.
We'd have found
something …'

I give his hand a gentle tug.

'But, ummmm …

Thanks.'

Can't Help but Like It

Dad says he can smell
that the Harts are good cooks –
and even though
he usually says,
We don't need nobody's help,
today Dad sighs
and says,
'I'm glad
I don't have to
think about cooking.'

What-if Worries

When we're nibbling
still-warm cheesy bacon muffins,
I tell Dad
how I waited
                    all alone.

'You didn't come
and you didn't come
and it was just me
for a long time
and I didn't know what to do.'

                    'I'm sorry baby-girl,'
                    Dad says.
                    'My head was all shook up
                    and I didn't even realise
                    school had finished.
                    I didn't make much sense at all
                    for a while there.'

'I was watching,
                waiting,
                    worried for so long

                            until Tahnee found me.'

I feel the worry
welling up,
squeezing my heart
            again.

'What if it happens
and we're not at this place
where we have

friends?'

What About Next Time?

'Awww, Lucy,'
Dad chokes out,
bundling me into his arms
as we sit
on the edge of
his bed.

'We were
doing okay,
just you and me.'

I nod.
Feel my head rub
against his chest
and bump his chin.

My eyes
blur with tears.

I love Dad and me –
but ...

'I don't want to be
                    alone
again,'
        I whisper.

'And I

don't want to

move

anymore.'

Tangled Web

Dad doesn't answer.
Just holds me,
running his fingers
through my no-knots
Mrs-Hart-helped-brush-it
hair, as tears trickle
down my cheeks.

'I like this place, Dad.

I like the people, too.

Why do we have
to keep
          moving?'

Help Me Understand

At first,
Dad doesn't answer.
I wonder if he
didn't hear me …
Then I hear him swallow,
like there's a big lump
blocking his throat.

'When your mum died …'

        There's a long silence
        but I wait …

'I didn't know how to be
a good dad to my baby girl –
            to you –
all by myself.'

        I want to tell Dad
        he's always a good dad.
        But he takes a breath
        and keeps going.

'I was lost
without your mum.

Her parents …
they tried to help …
and they did …
at first …

But then,
they wanted you with them
more and more.'

Dad takes a shuddery breath.
Whooshes air out.

I find his hand
and hold on tight
like I'm his anchor,
but he's mine, too.

'I was scared
they'd want you
to live with them –
forever.'

Gasp.

Dad squeezes my shoulder
but keeps talking.

'Your mum was gone.

It was just you and me, Lucy.

What if I lost you, too?'

Dad and I
hug in a huddle
for the longest time.

'But, Dad …'
I whisper,

'What if they were
just trying to

help?'

Help Is at Hand

Dad moans
and stretches out on his bed –
I remember that he's been
hurt.

'Will you be all right?'
I worry.

I'm already thinking
that I will call Mei-hui
if Dad is sick
again.

'I'll be fine, Lucy,'
Dad murmurs.
'Just need to
lie down for a bit.'

I still have lots of questions –
but Dad needs to rest,
and my head is full of
thinking.

I get my backpack.
Study my plan
for a toad scoop.

Draw another plan
that might work
better.

But doesn't.
My head is too messy
to make sense of
toad scoops.

When Dad starts snoring softly,
I crawl up onto the bed
and into his cuddle.

Maybe, Mei-hui?

When I wake up,
I ask Dad if I can
stay home
and look after him,

but Dad says
I've got school
and he just needs
to rest.

Together we pack
my lunch
with snacks
from Mrs Hart.

I wonder
if Tahnee's lunch
will look like mine again.

I brush my hair
carefully,
like Mrs Hart showed me,
and Dad helps me
pull it into
a ponytail.

‘You feeling better now?’
Mei-hui asks Dad,
as we walk past the office.

Dad nods.
‘The doctor says to
rest today, but I should be
right for work on Monday.’

‘Maybe I can
pick Lucy up, sometimes,
if you need me?’
Mei-hui says.

Dad doesn’t answer
straightaway –
and when he does,
it’s like he’s sifting through words.

‘Yeah …
Maybe …
That’s
good to know.

Thanks,
Mei-hui.’

arrest the pest

Steps to Success

On Monday, Dad
is ready for work
again.

'Promise me you won't
be climbing
any ladders,'
I say.

But Dad says he promises
he'll check the ladder is secure
before climbing it.

Pin-up Pest

At lunchtime,
Roxie wants Tahnee
to make posters
advertising
Toad Busters.

'Can we help?'
Pia asks.

Roxie scrunches her nose,
starts to shake her head,
but Tahnee says,
'Of course!
We'll all make posters.

Come on, Lucy.

You too.'

Mei-hui Musters Up

'What is a toad buster muster?'
Mei-hui asks, pointing to the poster
I'm hanging on the van park noticeboard
after school on Tuesday.

I tell Mei-hui
how we want to
help the environment.

'It says to *Arrest the pest!*
How are you going to arrest
a toad, Lucy?'

'We're catching them,'
I say.

'And I can come?'
Mei-hui asks.
'To arrest this pest?'

Mei-hui is smiling at me,
her eyes a question
as I nod
and smile back.

'Yes. You can come.'

I tell her
how we're making
scoops
to catch toads.

'I will take grabbers,'
Mei-hui says,
making *chomp, chomp, chomp*
actions with her fingers.

The Scoop on Scoops

'Dad, I need to make
my scoop,'
I say when I get back to
our caravan.
'It's for homework.'

Dad thinks my plan
has potential –

'But toads hop,'
Dad says.

'What is stopping
your toad hopping
out?'

I didn't think
about that!

Caught!

On Friday,
we each have to show our scoop
and talk about
the design
and how it was made.

I don't like
talking in front of
the whole class.
All middle session,
I sit to the side
with my head
down,
hoping Miss Darling
won't notice me.

Later, I sneak a peek at
the clock.
Nearly bell time.

My shoulders start to relax.

'Lucy …'

I freeze.
Stare hard at
the smudge of dirt
on my knee.

'You're the last one
to share,'
Miss Darling says.

I try to look up,
but my body is frozen.

'Can I see your scoop, Lucy?'
Miss Darling says, moving towards
where I'm sitting.

She reaches down,
picks up my scoop.

'This looks interesting.
What does this piece do?'

    ...

        'And how many milk bottles
        did you use?'

            ...

                'And what part do you think
                you did best?'

I mumble.
Short bites.
Look at my shoe,
my scoop,
the carpet …

Until I'm saved
by the
bell.

Pests and Guests

Mei-hui meets us
at the gateway to
our secret garden,
then we walk through
the parklands
together.

Roger
is waiting at a picnic table
with a sign-up sheet.

Dad writes our names,
as more and more
of my classmates
arrive …

The park lights flicker on.

Roger points people
to disposable gloves
and protective eyewear.

'Before we start,
I just want to remind you:
toads are pests
but

we don't support
any activity that causes
suffering.

Now, let's catch cane toads!'

'All right!' Jack says.

List of Available Equipment

- ☑ disposable gloves
- ☑ protective eyewear
- ☑ plastic bags
- ☑ handwash
- ☑ first-aid kit

Catch of the Day

Roxie: *Yay.* My scoop actually works.

Jack: This scoop is useless! I'm using gloves.

Heidi: *Eeeek!* It hopped on my shoe.

Kody: Naww, Mum. He promised he'd come.

Michael: Jack! I was going to get that one.

Sara: Michael, there's one right at your foot!

Tahnee: I like your scoop, Miss Darling.

Ashton: I've got loads of toads!

Pia: Lucy's scoop works the best!

Lucy: Grab it, Mei-hui!

Miss Darling: I thought kids kept me hopping!

We Loop

We group.
  We troop.
    We swoop.
      We scoop.
        We *whoop!*

We nab a knot
    (a lot!)
of toads.

jump to conclusions

Dad Does Something New

On Monday,
Miss Darling gets a message
from the office.

Dad will be late.
Mei-hui will meet me
at the pick-up gate.

What's happened to Dad?
I wonder.

And what if Mei-hui
can't find me?

Or forgets?

Catching On

'How is the little
toad buster?'
Mei-hui asks,
helping me shrug into
my backpack.

She didn't forget!

I tell her how everyone
(even Jack and Kody)
wants to keep finding
ways to help.

'No-one wants to stop!'

As we walk, Mei-hui tells me
about her idea to organise
a toad buster muster
at the van park.

'We need to arrest the pest, too,'
she says.

'You think the other park kids
would like to help?'

I do.

And I would like to
walk to the amenities
without stepping on
a toad!

Cooking Up a Treat

Mei-hui has afternoon tea
snacks in her office.
We nibble
as we work.

First, Mei-hui
and I make a flyer
for the residents,
advertising the
toad buster muster.

Then, Mei-hui photocopies
one for each site,

and I slip the flyers into
the residents' mailbox slots.

When Dad still isn't home,
Mei-hui says I can help her
cook wonton soup
for dinner.

    I've never made
    wonton soup.

    I've never even
    tasted it.

I wonder why Dad is taking
so long –

but Mei-hui says,
'We won't worry.
Your dad knows Lucy is safe
with Mei-hui.'

But how do we know
that *Dad* is safe?

Takeaway

When Dad collects me
from Mei-hui's house-behind-the-office,
he's quiet.

Thinking …

Mei-hui gives Dad a container
of wonton soup.

'Your Lucy helped make it
so we will share – yes?

She is a good helper.'

'You didn't have to
make tea for us,'
Dad says,
'but, ummm …
thanks, Mei-hui.'

'I told Mei-hui
that I can make sausage pie,'
I tell Dad, as we walk to
our caravan.
'Maybe next time,
we can share with her.'

'Hmmmm …'

Shlurp!

'Do you like it?'
I ask,
slurping another
mouthful of wonton soup.

I love the taste.

'Hmmmm …'
Dad licks his lips.

But even though Dad answers,
it feels like he
isn't really here
with me.

Like he's …

Oh no!

My stomach flops
and I can't eat
anymore.

Is Dad making plans
to leave?

Is that why Dad was late?

Is that why he is so distracted?

Snail-slow

While Dad is at the shower,
I make sure Snail
is ready.

'I don't want to go, Snail,'
I whisper,
feeling like a stodgy glob
of squidgy putty – with all my
happiness squished out.

I pack some
special things in the
snail-print bag that
Mrs Hart said I could keep:

- my snail-print beeswax wrap
- the recipe for sausage pie
- a note from Tahnee
- my yo-yo.

I think about getting
the happy-rock snail
I painted –
but maybe Mei-hui
will see it
and remember me
like I'll remember Mei-hui.

If we're leaving,
I have one last job to do.
I get Dad's pen
and some old pizza flyers,
then sit at the table
and start to write.

.

.

.

'Lucy. It's past bedtime,' Dad says,
stepping into the caravan.
'What are you doing?'

He picks up the old pizza flyers
I used for my messages to
Mei-hui …

♡ Thank you
Mei-hui. ♡

Miss Darling …

You are the best
teacher. ✿

and Tahnee …

Snail knows I'm slow … 'cause I don't want to go.

'Where are you going?' Dad puzzles.

I look at Snail

and my snail-print bag
packed, ready,
near the caravan door.

At my notes
on the table.

And Dad,
his face scrunched in
confusion.

'I'm going with you,'
I tell Dad,
'but they're my
friends
and I want to say
goodbye.'

No Room for Friends

Next time \ /
I'm gonna be like Snail.
I won't let anyone squeeze
inside my shell again.
Saying goodbye hurts too much.

Time Is Up

My eyes burn
as Dad slides into the seat
opposite me.

'Maybe it's time, Lucy,'
Dad says softly.

I sniff,
take a deep breath,
as Dad reaches across
the table
and grips my hand,
a small smile
lighting his eyes.

'Maybe it's time

to stay.'

sending down roots

Pick a Place

Dad says the bump on his head
gave him lots to think about –
and picking fruit gives him
lots of time
to think.

He says there's
a job going at the orchard.
A permanent job. He talked
to his boss this afternoon.
After work. That's why
Dad was late.

And why
he was
distracted.

I Hope They Pick YOU

'I don't know if I've got it, yet,'
Dad cautions, as I throw
my arms around him.
'I wasn't going to say anything
until I knew.'

'If you don't get   this job,
you could find   another one,'
                    I tell him.
'We could still   stay.'

'I've been thinking
the same thing, Lucy-Lou,'
Dad says,
and I squeal –
                    '*Shhhh …*'
– and start to bounce around
the caravan table –
                    '*Lucy. People are sleeping.*'
– knocking Dad's phone –
                    CLUNK!
– and my notes,
onto the floor.

'If we're going to stick around,'
Dad says, bundling me into my bed,
'I think we'll need a bigger van.'

'With a bathroom?'

Permanent

Mei-hui says she hopes
we can stay in her van park
'for a long, long time'.

'You help.
        I help.
                Lucy helps.
We all help each other,'
she tells Dad.

Our Seed Is Sprouting

We
aren't
just a seed
anymore.
/
Dad |
tells me |
about uncles |
and aunts and |
cousins … |
\ |
| and
| our tree is
| growing.
| /
|
|

'Can we go see them?' I ask Dad.

'I hope so, Lucy,' Dad says,
his eyes distant and sad.
'One day …'

A Mummy-look

All week
as we're walking to school,
playing in the parklands,
getting ready for bed –
I ask …
and Dad talks about …
my mum.

The more he tells me,
the more I want to know,
the more Dad remembers …
and smiles.

He even shows me
my mum's picture.

'You look like her,
Lucy,' Dad murmurs,
'with those big blue eyes …'

Now,
when I'm brushing my hair,
I think maybe I can see her
in the mirror,
looking back at me.

I Pick YOU

On Friday,
when Dad meets me
at the pick-up gate
he is grinning
like a wide-mouthed frog.

Dad got the job!

Helping Out After School

Now that Dad works
longer days,
Mei-hui collects me
after school
and I:

- help Mei-hui
- do my homework
- share secrets with Snail
  as we trail through gardens
- join in some of the
  games with the other park kids.

> 'You should walk home from school
> with us,' they say.

Maybe one day I will …

I Heart the Harts

Some days
I go to Tahnee's house and us three
girls make things: craft, construction, costumes,
fun … friends … forever. Other times we meet
at the parklands, Dad and me and the Harts,
sometimes Mei-hui, too; stretching
out like a small tree as we
talk, eat, play and
be.

Just Perfect

It's just Dad and me
            (and Snail)
but, we're not
alone anymore.

And Snail knows
I like that.

Acknowledgements

Julie, our A4 sheet of crisscrossing unit planning all those years ago didn't just produce a fabulous integrated term of work … it grew into this book. Thanks to Bec, who first saw the story potential, Dee, who helped resolve swirling plotlines, and Linda, who volunteered feedback when self-confidence was in a downward spiral.

To the wonderful team involved in making and marketing this book: editors, designers, typesetters, publicists … Your attention to detail is always appreciated! Mandy, I adore Lucy. And Snail.

My own 'Lucy' was in my first class for a brief time. I've never forgotten her …